W9-BHU-021

Dear Parents and Educators,

Welcome to Penguin Young Readers! As parents and educators, you know that each child develops at his or her own pace—in terms of speech, critical thinking, and, of course, reading. Penguin Young Readers recognizes this fact. As a result, each Penguin Young Readers book is assigned a traditional easy-to-read level (1–4) as well as a Guided Reading Level (A–P). Both of these systems will help you choose the right book for your child. Please refer to the back of each book for specific leveling information. Penguin Young Readers features esteemed authors and illustrators, stories about favorite characters, fascinating nonfiction, and more!

I Brought My Rat for Show-and-Tell and Other Funny School Poems

LEVEL 3
GUIDED READING LEVEL M

This book is perfect for a **Transitional Reader** who:
- can read multisyllable and compound words;
- can read words with prefixes and suffixes;
- is able to identify story elements (beginning, middle, end, plot, setting, characters, problem, solution); and
- can understand different points of view.

Here are some **activities** you can do during and after reading this book:
- Reading Aloud: Poetry is a great way to teach children to learn and love language and reading. The poems in this book have a meter, or basic rhythmic structure, that is catchy. Take turns reading the poems aloud with the child. Be sure to pause when there's a comma and stop when there is a period.
- Vocabulary: Some of the words in this book may be unfamiliar to the child. Find the words below in the text. Look up the definitions of the words below and any other words the child does not understand.

bellowed	hunch	seething	tackling	threaten
commotion	limerick	scurried	tattoo	vexed

Remember, sharing the love of reading with a child is the best gift you can give!

—Bonnie Bader, EdM
   Penguin Young Readers program

*Penguin Young Readers are leveled by independent reviewers applying the standards developed by Irene Fountas and Gay Su Pinnell in *Matching Books to Readers: Using Leveled Books in Guided Reading*, Heinemann, 1999.

To my granddaughters,
Kelly and Brittany, with love—JH

For Bill, my city slicker sweetie—MS

Penguin Young Readers
Published by the Penguin Group
Penguin Group (USA) Inc., 375 Hudson Street, New York, New York 10014, USA
Penguin Group (Canada), 90 Eglinton Avenue East, Suite 700, Toronto, Ontario M4P 2Y3, Canada
(a division of Pearson Penguin Canada Inc.)
Penguin Books Ltd, 80 Strand, London WC2R 0RL, England
Penguin Ireland, 25 St Stephen's Green, Dublin 2, Ireland (a division of Penguin Books Ltd)
Penguin Group (Australia), 707 Collins Street, Melbourne, Victoria 3008, Australia
(a division of Pearson Australia Group Pty Ltd)
Penguin Books India Pvt Ltd, 11 Community Centre, Panchsheel Park, New Delhi—110 017, India
Penguin Group (NZ), 67 Apollo Drive, Rosedale, Auckland 0632, New Zealand
(a division of Pearson New Zealand Ltd)
Penguin Books, Rosebank Office Park, 181 Jan Smuts Avenue, Parktown North 2193, South Africa
Penguin China, B7 Jaiming Center, 27 East Third Ring Road North,
Chaoyang District, Beijing 100020, China

Penguin Books Ltd, Registered Offices: 80 Strand, London WC2R 0RL, England

Library of Congress Control Number: 2003015058

ISBN 978-0-448-43364-6   10 9 8 7 6 5 4 3 2 1

PENGUIN YOUNG READERS

LEVEL 3

TRANSITIONAL READER

I Brought My Rat for Show-and-Tell

and Other Funny School Poems

by Joan Horton

illustrated by Melanie Siegel

Penguin Young Readers
An Imprint of Penguin Group (USA) Inc.

Contents

I Brought My Rat for Show-and-Tell.......6

Cafeteria Food...10

How to Do Your Homework....................12

Brenda..16

The Classroom Party....................................17

Mrs. Hall's Instructions
  for the Class Picture..................................18

Thanksgiving Play...22

Poetry Assignment......................................26

Snow Day...27

Christopher's Math Test..............................28

What I Tell the Bully................................30

Harvey..32

Homework Paper......................................36

Valentine's Day......................................38

Answer, Please.......................................40

Principal's Intercom Announcement......42

The Monster in Our Classroom................44

Bubble Gum Rap.....................................46

I Brought My Rat
for Show-and-Tell

I brought my rat for show-and-tell

For everyone to see,

But when I stood before the class,

He got away from me.

This caused a big commotion

As he scurried all about.

Kids were jumping up on chairs,

And some began to shout.

"Calm down," the teacher hollered.

"Enough of this, I say."

Just then my rat raced at her;

She fainted dead away.

I brought my rat for show-and-tell.

I made a big mistake.

I'll never bring my rat again.

Instead, I'll bring my snake.

Cafeteria Food

Wednesday is spaghetti day.

I bought a heaping mound,

And right before my very eyes

It started wiggling 'round.

Through the sauce the pasta crawled.

I stared in dumb surprise

To find it staring back at me

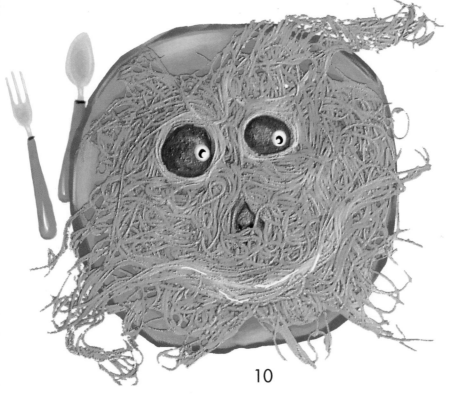

With two big meatball eyes!

I think this food is pretty weird.

What's more, I have a hunch

That every Wednesday from now on

I'd better bring my lunch.

How to Do Your Homework

Open your notebook

and lie on the floor,

Prop up your feet on the chair.

Look at the first set of questions,

Complain the assignment's not fair.

Cover your pencil with bite marks,

Admire the pattern they make,

Doodle all over your paper,

Decide that it's time for a break.

Call up a kid in your class,

Brag that you got a tattoo.

He'll tell you he doesn't believe you,

Pretend that it's perfectly true.

Jump up and down on your bed,

Get bored and pester your brother.

Threaten to give him a noogie,

Stop when he yells for your mother.

Shine a flashlight through
your fingers,
Figure out why they turn red.
Think about tackling the questions,
But play with your Game Boy instead.
Make up a dozen excuses,
Pick out the very best one
To give to your teacher tomorrow
When she asks why your homework's
not done.

1. ~~Dog~~
2. Stomachache
3. Viking plunder
4. Broken lamp
5. Flood

Brenda

On Monday, Brenda tweaked my ear.

On Tuesday, she stomped my toes.

On Wednesday, she kicked both
my shins.

On Thursday, she socked my nose.

But Friday was the darkest day

Of my entire week.

That's when Brenda grabbed me

And kissed me on the cheek.

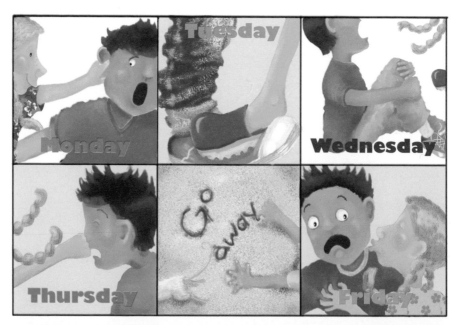

The Classroom Party

As fast as he could, Lumpy Orr

Was wolfing down cupcakes galore.

What happened next

Left the janitor vexed

And Lumpy with room

for lots more.

Mrs. Hall's Instructions
for the Class Picture

"Randy and Zack, tall kids in back,

Christy and Brian, change places.

Harvey and Heather, move closer

together,

Darius, stop making faces.

"Kelly and Blair, smooth down your hair,

Ronnie, stop wrestling with Ned.

Sarah, don't fidget.

What is it, Bridget?

Who's making ears on your head?

"No bubble gum, Kate,

And stop shoving, Nate.

Honestly, you are the limit.

Geraldo, I know

That you gotta go,

But couldn't you hold it

one minute?

BOYS

"The photographer's ready,

Uncross your eyes, Freddy,

Everyone smile and say,

CHEESE!

"Jenny Lynn Prime,

This isn't the time

To pick at the scabs on your knees.

20

"Let's try again.

What happened to Ken?

Randy, move back to the rear.

Thank goodness," she said,

With a shake of her head,

"Class pictures are just once a year."

Thanksgiving Play

Mrs. Hall assigned us parts
In our Thanksgiving play,
The one our class is putting on
Tonight for the PTA.

I hoped I'd be a pilgrim
Just like Jeffrey, Sue, and Grant,
Or else the friendly Squanto
With his gift of corn to plant.

But when I saw the part I got,

I groaned, "Wow, what a bummer.

Why can't we skip November

And fast-forward right to summer?"

But here I am in costume.

Mrs. Hall says I look perky.

I only wish I weren't the one

She picked to play the turkey.

Poetry Assignment

I'm having a terrible time,

I never will learn how to rhyme,

There must be a gimerick

To writing a limerick,

I can't even think of one line.

Snow Day

"Hooray, hooray! Hooray, hooray!
It snowed last night; no school today."
Cheers ring out all over town
As girls and boys jump up and down,
But the loudest cheer of them all
Is from their teacher, Mrs. Hall.

Christopher's Math Test

Eight pears plus three more is ten,

Twelve minus nine equals two,

Take one dozen apples from six

dozen more

And the total is still quite a few.

Seven times seven is seventy-seven,

Five into thirty is four.

These are the answers he put on his test,

And zero was Christopher's score.

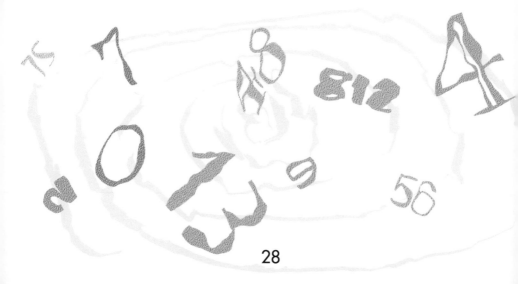

NAME Christopher

= 10

12 − 9 = 2

1 DOZ

= 541

7 × 7 = 77

5)30 = 4

29

What I Tell the Bully

So what if you are mean and tough

And trip kids in the hall,

And have the biggest muscles—

I'm not scared of you at all.

You're a dweeb, a dork, a doofus,

A gigantic ugly pox,

A reject from the planet,

And you smell like stinky socks.

You walk like a gorilla
With your knuckles on the ground,
And, fungus face, you'd better not
Try pushing *me* around
'Cause your brain's a whole lot smaller
Than those cooties on your head.

That's what I tell the bully
When I'm safe at home in bed.

Harvey

I'm not as good at playing ball
As Michael, Chris, or James,
So no one ever picks me first
When choosing sides for games.

When teaming up for spelling bees,

Kids look at me and pass

Till I'm the only one who's left

In our entire class.

I'm in the slowest reading group,

I lag behind in races

As other runners beat me

By at least 100 paces.

I hope someday when I grow up,

I'll come in first, not last.

Meanwhile, I am hoping

That I grow up really fast.

Homework Paper

When he saw my homework paper,

Dad was positively sore.

"An F in math?" he bellowed

With a loud, resounding roar.

He was madder than a hornet,

He was in a purple rage

As he paced about the kitchen

Like a tiger in a cage.

"For the life of me," he hollered,

"I don't see how this can be.

Why, I was always good in math,"

My dad reminded me.

When he saw my homework paper,

Dad was seething to the core.

I guess this means he'll never

Do my homework anymore.

Valentine's Day

They're passing out valentines.

Tasha's got two

And Cindy and Caitlin

Have got quite a few.

There's another for Simon

And several for Jenny,

A big one for Marcus,

And three more for Kenny.

And here's one for Tina,

A red heart with lace,

The one that she sent

To herself—just in case.

Answer, Please

Whenever I'm bouncing clear out
of my chair,
Eagerly waving my hand in the air,
The teacher pretends I'm not even there.
But if she asks, "Where is Kalamazoo?"
And I don't know the answer
and haven't a clue,
I can count on her calling
on you-know-who.

So here is my plan. Starting today,

I'll simply behave in the opposite way.

If I'm sure of the answer, I'll make

myself small,

And if I'm not, I'll sit really tall.

Principal's
Intercom Announcement

"Girls and boys, attention, please.

Good morning. This is Mr. Pease.

The math test scheduled for today

Is canceled, and I'm pleased to say

I'm now excusing everyone

Who didn't get his homework done.

"For those of you who buy your lunch,
Instead of beans and cabbage crunch,
They're serving chocolate cake supreme
With triple ripple fudge ice cream.

"And one thing more before I go.
There's something all of you should know.
Tomorrow, there'll be no more school.
Only kidding."

April Fool!

The Monster in Our Classroom

The monster quickly gobbled up the letters A-B-C,

Then polished off the alphabet, including X-Y-Z.

"A most delicious meal," he sighed,

And settled back quite satisfied

Till B-U-R-P gave a shout

And hollered, "Hey you, let us out."

The monster murmured, "Pardon me,"

Then opened wide and set them free.

Bubble Gum Rap

Blew a bubble, didn't stop,

Bigger, bigger, bigger—pop!

Teacher turned, saw the bubble,

Heard the pop, double-trouble.

Quickly blew one bubble more,

Bigger than the one before.

Started floating off my chair,

Past the teacher, through the air,

Soaring skyward with my bubble

Far away from double-trouble.

Teacher gasped and cried, "How weird!"

Right before I disappeared.

The End